MW01488882

Learning How To F.L.Y.

Learning How To F.L.Y.

First Love Yourself

Loco Fab

Copyright © 2019 by Loco Fab.

Library of Congress Control Number:		2018913672
ISBN:	Hardcover	978-1-9845-6649-2
	Softcover	978-1-9845-6648-5
	eBook	978-1-9845-6647-8

All rights reserved. No part of this book may be reproduced or transmitted in any form or by any means, electronic or mechanical, including photocopying, recording, or by any information storage and retrieval system, without permission in writing from the copyright owner.

This is a work of fiction. Names, characters, places and incidents either are the product of the author's imagination or are used fictitiously, and any resemblance to any actual persons, living or dead, events, or locales is entirely coincidental.

The views expressed in this work are solely those of the author and do not necessarily reflect the views of the publisher, and the publisher hereby disclaims any responsibility for them.

Any people depicted in stock imagery provided by Getty Images are models, and such images are being used for illustrative purposes only.
Certain stock imagery © Getty Images.

Print information available on the last page.

Rev. date: 02/15/2019

To order additional copies of this book, contact:
Xlibris
1-888-795-4274
www.Xlibris.com
Orders@Xlibris.com
787241

CONTENTS

I dedicate this book to my Lord and Savior, Jesus Christ, for giving me the vision, transparency, strength, and creativity to write this after twenty years. I also want to thank everyone who encouraged me and those who tried to tear me down. For when I was weak, God made me strong.

Epigraph

As children, we're so innocent, and it's so beautiful. I've found when the Lord has a great calling on your life, the enemy starts attacking you as early as possible. He will use anything and anyone.

For example, someone whom you look up to might have called you fat, and that sticks with you for the rest of your life.

Another example, you get molested as a child, and your innocence is automatically taken away and replaced with shame and multiple insecurities that follow you throughout your adulthood.

Prologue

I went to college and joined a grief therapy group and met some of the most amazing girls ever! We all shared our life stories as a means of healing. Being transparent is definitely a source of healing. We all had a lot in common. It was as if God created our little group for healing and sisterhood to strengthen one another and draw closer to him. We didn't judge one another. We loved one another. We still keep in touch on a regular basis.

I learned something from each of them, and I'm sure they learned some things from me also. I believe women should build one another up and not tear one another down over jealousy or some other petty reason. We're all beautiful in our own way. God said that we are "beautifully and wonderfully" made. So since the Creator of the universe says it, I believe it!

I have five very close friends, and we have shared our life experiences over the years. Paisley, Bam, Annie, Flores, Sasha, and I are lifetime friends. They have allowed me to share their stories to hopefully encourage others and save them from making some of the same mistakes that we made.

CHAPTER 1

Paisley

You would never look at Paisley and believe she had endured so much dysfunction. Most try to hide their truths, the essence of who they really are from trials that life has thrown to break them instead of make them. The enemy doesn't want us to be freed from guilt, shame, and pain because that's where our hang-ups end and healing begins.

Paisley had the kindest spirit and a heart of gold. She was beautiful, very talented, and everyone on campus loved her, except herself. She didn't even think she was beautiful or lovable! That just blew my mind because she was stunning! After hearing her story, I understood.

Of course, we all have a few people who dislike us no matter what, but that's only to let you know that you're doing something right! If everyone loves you, you're definitely doing something wrong.

Paisley was molested by multiple family members after her mother's tragic death at a young age. To cope with the hurt and loss, she began drinking at an early age, and the worst characteristic to get rid of was the "mask."

We've all worn one at one time or ten thousand, whether we know it or not. It's that fake voice that automatically retorts, "I'm great!" as soon as someone says, "How are you?"

Her parents went through a horrible divorce. She was very close with her mom. Paisley was the one her mom came to for advice and the first one whom her mom told when she got pregnant by another man who wasn't her husband.

Paisley was excited to have a sibling at first, then she realized that she wouldn't be the only child anymore. She became jealous and rebellious, which was out of character for her.

She was at the hospital with her mother and cousin when her baby brother was born. She wouldn't even look at him on the ride back home, even though he was strapped in his car seat right beside her.

As soon as they arrived home, she remembered her mom telling her to go over and look at her baby brother. She didn't want to, but she didn't want to seem jealous, although she admits she was. As soon as she laid eyes on him, she fell in love! He was the most beautiful baby she had ever seen. She said that he looked like a toy.

He never cried and always smiled at her. From that moment on, he became her baby. But after her mother's death, Paisley's life was never the same. That was how she ended up in the grief therapy group with the rest of us hurting souls—the six silly grief girls.

CHAPTER 2

Bam

My other friend Bam had a very similar childhood to Paisley's. Bam was tall and awkward. She had glasses and beautiful hair that she always kept in a ponytail. She didn't display any confidence, and it took her awhile to even open up to us. Her mother went through a lot when she was growing up. Her mom was also an alcoholic, but she didn't become an alcoholic overnight. There were multiple events, from accusations of her dad cheating on her mom to her mom being forced to get an abortion one year after Bam's birth.

Her mother never truly recovered from the abortion. In 1985, there were no places to go for help to deal with such a terrible loss. In her community, they didn't even know about therapists, counselors, or psychologists.

The only thing they had was the local preacher, and at that time, there was no point in reaching out to him.

The church building has to stop being a country club and a hospital for the sick. No one is better than anyone else. We are made from love to love. To hate others is unnatural. God is love.

Her mom was broken, and Bam didn't know how to help her mom. That was when her obsessive compulsive disorder (OCD) started. She started doing certain things as rituals to keep everyone in her family safe from death. She was constantly worried that something bad was going to happen.

This reminds me to watch what you think about. The Bible says perfect love removes fear. Fear comes from the enemy to steal our joy and take our peace. Remember, you bring about what you think about.

A year before her mother's death, Bam had a horrible dream. She woke up screaming and crying because it was so vivid and real.

The crazy thing is, everyone involved in her dream were the same people whom her mom visited the night she died—the night that Bam didn't pray for her!

Bam's life was forever changed. This was how she ended up in grief therapy with the rest of us bruised girls—the six silly grief girls.

CHAPTER 3

Annie

Annie was the shortest of the group. She was four feet ten but swears she's five feet. We know that's not true because Paisley is five feet, and she's slightly taller than Annie. She's still in denial.

Annie had the perfect hourglass shape, perfect teeth, and braces due to TMJ, and she was very optimistic. She was outgoing and a majorette for the band.

Annie recalled the night before her mother's death. Her mother had slapped her for letting someone ride her bicycle. She had never been slapped by her mom before. Later, she found out that her mom was upset because her dad didn't pick her up as usual. He had a new girlfriend, so her mom was hurting.

Annie understands now that she's an adult. When the one person you love more than anything rejects you, it's going to go one of two ways: the high road or the low one.

Unfortunately, her mom chose the low road.

Annie always knew God existed from a very early age. We all have that in common, which is nothing short of amazing!

Annie recalled that she couldn't even talk yet but knew he was watching over her. No one told her; she just knew God existed, and she loved him. She used to play by herself a lot in her room and talk to God all day.

Annie recalled the night her mother slapped her. She was so hurt that she decided she wasn't going to pray for her. She had a list of the whole family whom she would pray for every night for as long as she could remember. However, that particular night, she decided not to pray for her mama. She remembers just like it was yesterday; the Holy Spirit said, "If you don't pray for your mama, she might die." And Annie said aloud, "I don't care if she dies or not."

Of course, Annie was still hurting because her mom slapped her, but she didn't really think her mom would die! The very next day, she woke up, and her mom wasn't home. That was weird, but her loving grandmother got her ready for school, so it was no big deal, she thought.

She was in the cafeteria, being the class clown to mask the pain, when she looked up and saw her entire family (except her mama) standing in the front door of the cafeteria. The principal came over and asked her to come to the office. She had a sick feeling in her stomach.

Annie somehow knew that her mama was gone! She was signed out by someone. She was frantic! She kept asking, "Where is my mama?" Everyone had bloodshot eyes and no words. She just wanted to see her grandmother because she always made her feel better.

As soon she arrived at her grandmother's house in the projects (which she used to be embarrassed of but now loves because she had the best childhood memories there), there were a ton of people outside, screaming and crying. It still haunts her to this day.

Before she could get to her grandmother, her mama's only sister rushed up to her and said, "Your mama is dead!"

Annie collapsed. The next thing she remembered was someone taking her to her dad. She remembered knocking on the door, and when he opened it, she burst into tears and said, "Daddy, Mama is dead!" She didn't remember what happened after that for several months. I've found that the Lord protects us by removing hurtful memories.

Her mom was hit while walking to the store. They never found out who the driver who hit her was.

This is how Annie ended up in grief therapy with the rest of us bruised girls—the six silly grief girls.

CHAPTER 4

Flores

Flores was biracial. She never felt that she fit in with either the white girls or the black girls. She ended up attending an HBCU (historically black college and university) because she grew up in a town that was 95 percent white. She wanted to see what it would be like to be around the majority of blacks. She still felt out of place, until she joined the grief therapy group.

Flores had a tragic childhood also. She lost her mom to cancer when she was eight. She lived with her grandmother and several cousins. Her uncles and aunts were all on drugs, so her grandmother was left with raising everyone's children. She didn't really know her dad, but he was honorably discharged from the army to raise her.

Her father had several sisters located in the same small town of Smitten, Indiana, but none of them took an interest in her. Her mom was black and apparently from the other side of the tracks, so she wasn't good enough, or so it seemed.

This just confirmed all the negativity the enemy was overwhelming Flores with. Shame, guilt, the feeling of not being good enough—she felt ugly and disgusting, and she was sure that she was the reason her mama died!

Flores remembered being a brat. She didn't know her mom had cancer. No one told her that her mom was even sick. She regrets being a brat now. Losing her mother made her the most humble and caring person I've ever met. She was in shock! She was never taken to therapy or anything. She was expected to bounce back like nothing had happened. She lost her mama! To make it worse, she was taken away from her grandmother, who was basically her mama.

Before her parents were divorced, they used to party all the time while she lived with her grandmother. They would drop by every now and then and give her lots of gifts, but they'd soon be out the door. Somehow, she was okay with that because she had her grandmother.

Her dad would joke around and call her Thunder Thighs in front of her friends. That hurt her to her core. She even started wearing those thigh thinners to school. She had them on so tight that she literally had blisters on both thighs. Of course, she got in trouble for that.

Her mom was beautiful, very skinny, and perfectly shaped, with a natural sexy walk. Flores was chunky and awkward, and after her mom's death, she was talked about negatively by her dad on a regular basis. She had no one to turn to but God. He was always with her, and that gave her peace.

Parents can really jack up a child's life by not showing the proper affection, love, and affirmation that a child needs. These scars sometimes last a lifetime without the proper help.

His joking affected her and the decisions she would make going forward. For a girl not to have her mom in her life, with a dad who wanted a boy and was constantly tearing her down, is a disaster waiting to happen. This is how she ended up in grief therapy—the six silly grief girls.

CHAPTER 5

Sasha

Sasha was beautiful and made a size 14 look amazing. She had natural curly hair that flowed past her shoulders. She was very smart, but she played dumb to fit in. I told her she wasn't made to fit in; she was made to stand out. Like her friends, she had low self-esteem.

Be the person whom you need, and you'll feel like you're making a difference in someone's life. Isn't that what it's all about? If everyone would stop focusing on themselves and their problems and help others with their problems, the world would be a much better place. So many people are so selfish instead of selfless.

Sasha was molested by several family members and never told anyone until she joined the group. When she was growing up, she was miserable, but no one ever knew her pain. She masked it with jokes and made sure everyone was happy because she knew how it felt to be unhappy, and that wasn't going to happen to anyone on her watch. Her paternal grandfather had a storage house filled with all kinds of liquors. Starting in the seventh grade, Sasha would sneak out there and fill up a Big Gulp cup and drink it throughout the day at school.

No one had a clue! She even drove herself to school because she couldn't get dressed before the bus came because she was always hungover. Her dad had a yellow 1967 Impala. She's every bit of four feet ten at that time, so she had bed pillows and couch pillows helping her see above the steering wheel, without her dad's consent of course. He was at work.

Her friends started calling her Bus 29. The last school bus was 28, and she would roll up behind it and pick up her friends. She was in the seventh grade but had senior friends who helped her get access to a parking spot in the senior lot.

I will admit, her people skills are off the charts! She was voted wittiest for years, from elementary school through high school.

Sasha basically failed every class. She switched schools during the tenth grade and went from failing every class to becoming an honor student.

She felt the teachers there cared, which made her put in more effort and stop drinking during school. She loved it there!

There were only five black people in her class, but she never thought about it that way. You were either her friend or a mean person, because she befriended everyone. She was small in stature but would go off on a bully in a heartbeat!

She knew how it felt to be called names and be mistreated, and that simply wasn't going to happen in her presence. This was how she ended up in grief therapy—the six silly grief girls.

CHAPTER 6

Paisley's Breaking Point

Paisley was doing great in school and appeared to be the happiest and funniest chick ever, but on the inside, she was dying. She literally wanted to die. Her dad had a really sharp knife that he would sharpen every night. He would even show her how it could cut a sheet of paper in half with ease. That was when she decided to slit her wrists!

She was tired of living this fake life, which was nothing short of hell for her. She waited for him to go to work the next morning, and that was when she would follow through with her plan—so she thought.

She had watched her dad sharpen this knife every single night, so it had to be the one. She remembered she was sixteen, and she took the knife into her room and tried to cut her wrists! She literally sawed, but it would not cut! So she started pressing harder. It would burn, but nothing was cutting. So naturally, she tried the right arm. Still, she was unable to slice her wrists! She was dumbfounded. She didn't have a plan B on how to get out of this hell called life.

Paisley barely has scars now.

CHAPTER 7

Annie's First Love

Annie said that she would never forget her first love. She had never been into boys before because she was either kin to them or was not attracted to them. She met a guy from New York. She fell in love with him as soon as she laid eyes on him. Of course, now she realizes she just wanted to feel loved. That was where she went wrong.

When we're hurting and all we want is love, God is the only solution. A person can never give you the love God has for you. But at sixteen, Annie was convinced that he was the one (the first of many).

They dated throughout high school until she found out in a paper during her senior year that he was with another girl! The article said they had been together for two years!

She was in shock! She left school, went home, and started drinking. She passed out in the backyard, where her dad almost ran over her because he didn't see her. She thought she was going to marry this guy.

Back in the '90s, that was what was expected. You graduate in high school and then get married. Well, those plans were ruined.

One day, her friends asked her to take them into the city. She was from a small town. She was the only one who had a car.

Side note: I have to tell you about the car. It was a five-speed manual Toyota. Annie's dad tried to teach her how to drive it several times to no avail. He would start yelling at her, which only made her cry, and then he would become even angrier because she was crying. He would tell her, "Stop all that crying!" So eventually, she learned to stop crying.

He said she couldn't get her license until she learned how to drive that car! She was sixteen and in love, so she had to figure out a way. So as always, she prayed and asked God to help her. She didn't know how he would, but she had faith that he would, and that was all she needed!

Annie dreamed one night that she was driving that car the entire night! When she woke up, she ran into the living room and said, "Dad, I know how to drive a stick shift now! I've been driving all night!" He didn't hesitate to toss her the keys, and they headed out while she was still in her pajamas.

He jumped on his motorcycle and took off, and Annie was right behind him! She didn't stall once! They drove at least fifty miles, and she never messed up, not even on a steep hill with a car behind her! Needless to say, he was shocked, and she got her license the same week! (Shout out to God for being so awesome!)

Back to the story (sorry, I have ADD, and the meds apparently aren't working), two of her friends were getting their hair done and the other one was going to hang out with her boyfriend. That left her and another friend alone to figure out what they were going to do. They were both in love with jerks who didn't love them.

So they found a gallon of gin (brand-new) at the house of her friend's boyfriend. They left them there while they went to the mall, and she and her friend started drinking it with fruit punch. She literally couldn't taste any alcohol. Annie remembered leaving the house of her friend's boyfriend to go pick up their other friends from the salon, and she tripped and fell down the concrete stairs onto the sidewalk. She began to laugh so hard because it didn't hurt.

She felt no pain. She even started banging her head against the sidewalk because she couldn't understand why she couldn't feel any pain. She was like, "I told you, I'm a superhero!" The rest was a blur.

Apparently, Annie drove to her ex's house and had an emotional breakdown! He called her dad to come and get her. She was so out of it that her dad and uncle thought she was on drugs!

They took her to a local hospital, and she recalled the physician saying that she was lucky. Had she drank more, she could have become mentally damaged! She didn't even know that was possible. Of course, she was humiliated and completely embarrassed.

CHAPTER 8

Bam's First Love

I've learned when you didn't get the love and encouragement you needed as a child, you look for it from other people, mostly in intimate relationships. I didn't know then that you attract who you are, not who you pretend to be.

So if you're a jacked-up, insecure person, like we were, you're going to attract another jacked-up, insecure person. Well, Bam ended up marrying her first love behind her dad's back because her dad didn't like him, which made her like him even more. (We look back at some of the stupid choices we made because we were bruised—not broken—from childhood, and thank God for keeping us in our right minds through the drama and craziness.)

When you're raised in a dysfunctional household that becomes your norm, that's the kind of relationship you will feel most comfortable in because that's all you know. We're simply not attracted to guys who are stable, kind, and loving. That's not our norm, so it doesn't feel natural. How sad. We had to get a new normal, and quickly. Seriously, listen to your parents. They only want the best for you, even if they're jerks.

Bam had a fear of bumps for some reason. Her dad capitalized on that and told her if she had sex before marriage, she would break out in bumps all over! That freaked her out!

She told her then boyfriend that they needed to get married if they were going to have sex. He was crazier than she was and went along with it.

He had no money, so she bought the rings (red flag). She clearly heard the Holy Spirit speaking to her heart, saying, "Don't do this! He is not right for you!" Of course, she thought it was the devil trying to steal her joy. Boy was she wrong. He cheated on her literally three months to day after their secret marriage!

Every month, she would set out candles and have a romantic night planned on the eighteenth. This night was different. He played football for another university, but he should have been home hours ago. They had a quaint apartment, and she was so happy just to feel loved.

Suddenly, she knew he was with another woman. I can't tell you how important it is to have a relationship with God! The Holy Spirit will always warn you either before, during, or after something harmful or hurtful is about to happen.

Thankfully, he will also stop you in your tracks (that example will come later) from making really dumb decisions.

Bam was so heartbroken. She cried as she blew the candles out and got ready for bed. When he finally showed up, she confronted him and said, "I know you have been out cheating on me tonight! Who was it?"

She honestly didn't expect him to fess up so quickly, but he did! He started telling her everything that happened in graphic (and unnecessary) detail. She was even more hurt because this girl was the town whore. Literally, everyone had slept with her. Here she was, the good girl saving herself for marriage, and she was being cheated on with the town slut!

Of course, that did nothing for her self-esteem. She decided to leave him but found out a couple of weeks later that she was pregnant! She couldn't believe it, because she was diagnosed with endometriosis and adenomyosis in high school. She was told she most likely would never have children. But we know God has the last say-so!

The world was so horrible. She actually felt blessed not being able to have children. She began to think this was God's way of telling her to give him another chance—another mistake that could have been avoided had she prayed to God for an answer instead of making an emotional decision to stay in a toxic relationship.

When we're from dysfunctional families with bruises from childhood, we'll make up something to stay in an unhealthy relationship because we feel like this gives us validation. Someone loves you so you must be lovable, right? That's only short-term and, usually, conditional love.

We know now the only one who can fill the "God hole" is the one who made it.

When you're bruised as a child, the best thing to do is to get into a relationship with God and ask him to heal all the bruised spots in your life. You need to be whole and know your purpose before you should get married. Whoever God has for you will complement your purpose and vice versa. How can you marry someone when you don't even know who you are and what your purpose is? Otherwise, it's just two bruised and hurt people creating more dysfunctional situations for their own children, and the cycle continues.

CHAPTER 9

Paisley's First Love

Paisley was desperate for love just like the rest of us. She met a guy who appeared to have his act together. He owned several businesses. He was divorced but had a great relationship with his ex and took great care of his children. They dated for about a year, and she ended up pregnant. She couldn't have a baby without being married! She was so worried about what people would think. (Side note: The only one you should try to please is God, not people. God saves your soul. People will turn their back on you at a drop of a dime.)

She didn't have a clue about babies! She thought when a woman became pregnant, she could eat literally anything she wanted, and when the baby arrived, all the weight would go too.

We all know that sounds ridiculous, but Paisley literally had the mind of a Disney character at times. She gained eighty-one pounds! She was unrecognizable even to herself. She recalled looking at a Polaroid picture and asking, "OMG! Who is that?" And her cousin was like, "Um, that's you, Mommy." She was in denial.

She was three weeks overdue, and her obstetrician decided to induce the pregnancy. She weighed 198 pounds the day she checked into the hospital! She was still in denial. Before going to the hospital, she took it upon herself to go to the library and rent movies on having babies. That was a big mistake!

Yep, I said library because we didn't have the internet then. That sounds so insane when I say that. I'm so retro (but not old). As you can see, denial is deep in our souls.

So Paisley thought she was as prepared as she was going to be until several doctors rushed in and said that she needed an emergency cesarean! She didn't even know what that was!

Apparently, her blood pressure was dropping at an alarming rate, and the baby was in distress. She was freaking out. She was at the hospital all alone. She wasn't sure where her boyfriend was. He had started making comments about her weight early in the pregnancy. She had a complex and felt very unattractive. He would flirt with other women in her face, and she would put up with it just to have a companion. She actually thought they were going to get married.

Don't ever try to hold on to anything or anyone that God is trying to move out of your life. You will hold back your own blessings and possibly become ill from being in a toxic relationship.

It was all a blur, but I did remember being alone but telling them her "husband" was on his way so that Paisley didn't appear to be a statistic, a.k.a., a baby mama. She literally hated that term!

The next thing she remembered was waking up a couple of days later and seeing a baby in an incubator beside her bed that held a precious baby with a head full of hair in it! She began to rub her eyes because everything was so blurry. At first she thought she was dead! Guess who else was in the room? You guessed it: her pretend husband.

She knew she wasn't dead then because that would be hell, and she knew she was a believer in her Lord and Savior, Jesus Christ, so hell wasn't an option. She hit the red button for the nurse because she noticed the baby's name was the same as his dad's! That was not, in a million years, the name she had for him!

She would literally accept any name but that one. The nurse came in and informed her that while she was sedated a couple of days, the dad was allowed to name him. She looked at Paisley with a smile and said, "Well, you don't have to worry. Dad was here to save the day! It's already on his birth certificate, so there's nothing I can do. Do you need anything else?" Paisley wanted to say, "Yes, a gun to shoot dear father of the year with."

She just started crying. She quickly remembered that crying was for punks. That was how she was raised by her dad. So she sucked it up, put her mask on, and accepted the fact that she had to deal with it.

She had decided way before giving birth that she was going to breastfeed her baby. Mostly because it was the healthiest thing to do for the baby, and it didn't hurt that it was free!

Paisley was barely able to pay all the bills, but of course, she made too much money for any type of government assistance. She could not believe it. Why were all these people who didn't work getting free food and housing, but those of us who did work had nothing but our little checks (after all the taxes were taken out), which barely enabled us to get by?

Moving on . . . she realized this was going to be a long road. A couple of weeks after having her baby, she took him in for his first checkup and also to see her obstetrician.

He weighed seven pounds and eleven ounces. He was twenty-one inches long. Paisley asked the doctor when the other seventy-plus pounds was going to come off. She was shocked when the doctor said, "When you exercise and work it off!"

Paisley was devastated once again. All the years of being called fat and pumpkin head, not to mention her boyfriend couldn't seem to stop flirting and cheating on her with everyone. The lies the enemy had been whispering to her since she was a small child just started replaying in her head. She thought she was the scum of the earth (another lie Satan had instilled in her as a child). He knows if he can break us down mentally as children, we will most likely make horrible life decisions and will not ascertain our divine destiny.

CHAPTER 10

Flores's First Love

After college, Flores moved back to her hometown with a guy whom she met at school. They were engaged, and she was planning the wedding and was so happy. They ended up moving to a larger city because she was too embarrassed to live in her hometown. Everyone knew about him cheating on her, and most of the guys wanted to kick his butt!

About two years later, she met a really good friend at work, who became her best friend, who was concerned about her because she had lost so much weight. She didn't tell her or anyone else that she was illegally taking fen-phen when it was killing people! Not even us!

She remembered having chest pains as she popped another pill. So her friend took her to the doctor, and the physician came out, saying, "Congratulations! You're pregnant!" Flores lost it! She remembered the doctor saying, "I hope those are tears of joy!"

She could not understand how this was even possible because she was leaving him and taking with her their baby, who was almost two! They hadn't slept together for months. She was like, "This is impossible!" She eventually figured out that he had been drugging her!

She loved her firstborn so much that she really thought there was no way she could love another child as much as her first one. Her friend made an appointment for her to get an abortion. A couple of days before, she knew she couldn't go through with it. It made no sense!

Flores was barely making it with one child and had no idea how she was going to make it with a second one.

CHAPTER 11

The Choice

After finding out that she was indeed pregnant, Flores came to a place of peace. She knew she could not kill an innocent soul. She had faith that God would make a way like he always had.

She decided again that the reason for this pregnancy must be to stay in that miserable marriage to a man incapable of being faithful and not even financially stable for their family.

With swollen eyes, she told her husband that she was pregnant after arriving home from work. He was thrilled! She told him about the abortion, and he said it was up to her. Of course it was!

Everything was up to her—from paying the bills to paying for day care, to buying the groceries, and to being a good wife to him even though, in her eyes, he didn't deserve it.

Flores told her friend the next day at work that she wasn't going to go forward with the abortion nor was she leaving her husband to move in with her. She was a dear friend and was only trying to help her because she saw how depressed Flores was. She opened her home to Flores and her baby until Flores could find somewhere else to stay; however, she assured Flores that they could stay with her as long as she wanted, and Flores knew she meant that. They still love each other so much!

Several years later, that same friend got married and had a son. She named him the same name that Flores named her second son. That's so precious to me.

Her friend saw the sadness in her eyes, but she also understood and supported her. Flores stopped taking the fen-phen immediately and went to the same pediatrician whom she had for her first son.

She decided to eat healthy because she knew the weight wasn't coming off when the baby decided to exit her body. Flores wore her mask so well that she learned to believe the fake version of herself. She appeared to be so happy, still the comedian at work, and as always, beyond depressed about her life and the poor choices she had made. She worried that something would be wrong with her baby because she was depressed and was truly afraid of not having enough love to give to another child.

Her firstborn was rambunctious, hilarious, and a joy to be around; however, he had no Off button. She used to feel like she was going to lose her mind because he would be bouncing off the walls when she picked him up from day care, all the way until she lay down with him, said their prayers, and waited for him to fall asleep. She was so afraid that having another one would literally throw her over the edge.

Flores learned that once you have a cesarean, you have a choice on whether or not you'd like to try having the baby naturally or schedule a cesarean. She was sure that she wanted to have the baby naturally, until she arrived at her last appointment. She thought about all those movies, and she knew there was no way that she was going to be able to push a baby out and survive. The first one almost killed her because he got stuck in the birth canal. She didn't want to take a chance of dying for fear of leaving her babies here with their biological father.

CHAPTER 12

The Birth And Rebirth

Flores's firstborn arrived into this world on a Saturday morning. She scheduled the birth for her second son, who was also weeks overdue, on a Friday evening. Seems like boys just don't want to come out after talking with other moms (just an FYI).

He was born on a Saturday also. He weighed seven pounds and ten and a half ounces and was twenty and a half inches long. It was eerie how close he and his brother were in weight and length.

She would never forget the day of the prescheduled cesarean. They wheeled her into the operating room after giving her an epidural, so she was feeling no pain. She could feel them tugging to get him out. As soon as they pulled him out, her spirit went up to the ceiling! The only thing that was keeping her attached to her body was what felt like a cord in her back. She could literally look back and see her body, all the doctors, and even her baby.

She thought for sure that she was about to die! So she immediately started praying for God to please allow her to be a mother to her children in this horrible world. She kept praying, "Please, Lord, do not take me away from my children," and the next thing she knew, she quickly went back into her body!

She immediately looked over at her insignificant other and asked him if she died. Of course, he just looked at her like she was crazy and said nothing after shaking his head. When the nurse came around the curtain to let her know how her baby was doing, she asked her if she died. The nurse replied, "No, my dear. You were just under medication."

Flores swears that she floated out of her body, and I believe her. It's a scientific fact that energy never dies. We are energy. Once our spirit leaves our body, it has to go somewhere. I believe that once we die, our spirits leave our bodies and either goes up or down. Flores was being pulled up. Both her hands and both legs were being pulled up, and she felt the cord in her back keeping her attached to her body. Had that cord broken, she wouldn't be here today.

Doctors have to be very careful when pulling babies out of their mothers. There is a spiritual connection that can cause life-altering trauma to either mom or the baby, or both. Thankfully, everything was well with Flores and her baby, and she was glad to be alive!

This baby was different. He didn't cry. She thought something was wrong with him. They handed him to her. His eyes were wide open, and he smiled at her. She had an immense feeling of peace come over her instantly, and she fell in love all over again. How silly of her to think she could not love another child!

Her boys were complete polar opposites though. Her new baby was an introvert, and her older son was an extrovert. The baby never cried. When she would lay him down, he'd just lay there and look around until he fell asleep. She called the doctor because her firstborn was the total opposite. He talked early and walked early.

Flores's secondborn didn't start talking until he was two, and no one could understand him except her. He had the cutest speech impediment ever! He started walking when he was close to three, which had her really concerned. Turns out, this child was a genius! He loved to do math.

When she gave them treats, her oldest wanted a toy or game, but her younger son wanted a workbook! She thought that was so funny. He would sit by himself for hours and work on those books. She would literally have to tear him away from them to give him lots of hugs and kisses. She had to literally chase her firstborn down, pin him to the ground, and try her hardest to get a couple of kisses in before he got away!

CHAPTER 13

The Battlefield In My Mind

The enemy will never leave you alone if you're a believer in Christ, so just get used to it. That's why the Bible says we need to renew our minds daily with the Word of God and meditate on his promises. I know this now. I was oblivious in 1999.

That was the day I was at an all-time low. I remember day care was outrageous for a toddler and a baby. The cost of living wasn't bad, but day care was ridiculous. I wasn't making much money, but God always worked it out. We never went hungry and always had a roof over our heads.

I just started crying. I didn't know what to do. I had no money to get my car fixed and had no idea how I was going to be able to get to work. I remember getting the kids out of the back seat. I always took the baby out first because if I let my older son out, he would take off, and I mean he could have run for the Olympic team for babies, if there were such a thing!

I walked in the apartment, and my older son started running around, having a ball. He was convinced that he was a Chinese ninja. I will take some of the blame for that. I loved karate movies. We took him to see Mortal Kombat when he was like two weeks old. Bless his heart; he jumped out of his skin so many times. But the movie was awesome! Yeah, that's the perk of being a young parent with no common sense.

I laid my baby on the couch, and then I started crying. I didn't know where their dad was, and I had to cook and figure out how I was going to get to work the next day. Suddenly, I wanted to disappear.

I'll never forget—the TV was off, and the remote was on the floor. I picked it up and tried to toss it onto the couch opposite of my baby, but it hit the floor instead. Suddenly, there was a lady I've never seen on TV, and she was looking directly at me! The TV zoomed in on her face, and we locked eyes.

She said, "I know you feel overwhelmed and you just want to die! Jesus loves you, and he has an amazing future for you." I literally sat down on the kitchen floor and started crying my eyes out.

God hadn't forgotten about me! He still loved me! I was overjoyed and filled with hope for the future suddenly. I later found out her name was Joyce Meyer. I love that woman!

God literally used her to turn my frown right-side up and to change my mind-set. There were no more pity parties for me. God put me here on this earth for a reason, and suddenly, I knew what it was. It seemed impossible—it still does—but I know when God starts a good work in you, he will see it to completion.

I still don't know how it's going to happen, but I have faith that it will. And when it does, I'll be ready!

I called a friend to ask for a ride to work.

My dad came up to visit and said the car just needed to sit out in the sun. That made no sense to me, but I'm respectful of my dad. He pushed the car into a sunny spot while I steered it. It was a Saturday morning. I'll never forget.

The next day, I went outside just to see what would happen; mind you, the car was literally dead before. It wouldn't start. I thought it needed a new battery. I began to pray for a miracle.

God had brought me out of so many dark places before; I knew he had no limitations. I took the keys, turned the ignition, and the car started right up! I sat there and cried for at least thirty minutes. I was so happy!

God did it again! Faith activates God's power. When we pray in faith and believe without any doubt that God will do something, he will do it! I'm a witness to it several times.

You've already read some of it, but you'll get the gist as I continue along my journey. I had a housephone by then and called my friend and told her that I didn't need a ride on Monday because my car was working! We both screamed with joy and excitement!

She was truly a blessing during her season in my life. I have learned that people are in our lives for a reason, season, or lifetime. Nothing could be truer!

CHAPTER 14

The Job Promotion

I was in customer service for an international company. I decided to take a chance on a job that literally paid double what I was making. God is in control of promotions anyway, and I knew anything was possible with the faith that I had.

The job description sounded really complicated, but I knew I could do all things through Christ who strengthened me!

I was called in for an interview. Somehow, I had so much confidence that I was going to get this job. I remember it was raining cats and dogs. We had two locations, and this job was located downtown, which was unfamiliar territory for me.

I literally worked, went to church, and went home every single day. That was all I knew. I made it into the interview soaking wet! I was a mess.

Remember, nothing you've been through shall be wasted! God has a purpose for each one of his children. We can do it the hard way, which complicates our lives and is literally a waste of time, followed by years of pain, or we can be patient and follow his will for our lives and not our own.

But when you've been bruised from childhood, it's hard to wait on God because you crave the love and affection that you didn't receive, at least I did.

I completed the interview and didn't feel like I did a good job. I was a mess, my hair was ridiculous, and I felt like I was not qualified for the position after interviewing with the management team.

I had decided that everything would be okay either way. At least I tried. The next day, HR called me and offered me the job! I was absolutely beside myself with joy. God came through big-time (again)!

The downside to it was that I was leaving the friends I had made over the years, who were more like family, because they weren't located in the downtown office. But the Lord knows that we needed the extra money!

So I started my new job and discovered it was way more difficult than the job description. It was very technical and analytical. It was very similar to an IT position. I remember the entire training class would whisper whenever the trainers stepped out, "Do you have any idea of what this job is?"

We all shook our heads no and laughed quietly. It was very professional, so I couldn't be my silly self that I was used to being in the other office, which was more relaxed. Once again, God gave us the best trainers! They were amazing and are still my close friends nearly fifteen years later!

They made everything so easy to understand, which was nothing short of a miracle if you knew all we were responsible for. I almost get anxiety thinking about it.

Moving right along, the job paid great, and I was paid for overtime too!

The downside was I never spent time with my boys. I left the house for work when it was dark, and when I arrived home after ten o'clock every night, they would be sleeping. But we had our weekends! I felt so guilty, but I knew I needed to take care of my children, so I had to make sacrifices that were out of my control.

I was in that role a decade before I was allowed to accept another position in the company back at my old location! I was thrilled! It was a promotion, but not really. It was a salaried position, and that meant I didn't get paid for overtime, but I was able to spend more time with my boys. There were no complaints from me.

CHAPTER 15

The Divorce

Paisley's marriage lasted twelve long years, and she literally couldn't take it anymore. She could not stand to look at her spouse. She was afraid that her children would become statistics because we all knew that there were fewer black families with both parents than without.

Her children were old enough at that point to stay at home by themselves, so she no longer needed a babysitter.

She walked in the door and was rushed with hugs and kisses from her babies, as always (it made her feel like a million dollars), and she asked them if it would be okay if they left their dad.

Her older child said, "Like a divorce?"

Paisley held her head down, waiting for them to start crying, and quietly said, "Yes, like a divorce." They all yelled with joy! She fell down because she was squatting while waiting for them to fall apart. She looked at her youngest daughter and said, "So you're okay with this?"

Her daughter quickly said, "Yes, ma'am!"

Her oldest son asked, "When are we leaving?"

She said, "Saturday!" This was a Thursday, so she had two days to make this happen. Of course, that would be all God because she couldn't do anything but mess stuff up without him. They all jumped up and down. It was one of the best days of her life!

Paisley filed for a divorce the next day. Mind you, she bought the house that they lived in when she was twenty-three, but her spouse refused to leave. The judge told her that she and the children needed to vacate the premises because he could not make her soon-to-be ex-husband move out because they had been married for so long.

She could not believe it! But God is so merciful. She immediately started looking for places to move to and found one on the same day! She didn't break her promise to her children. They moved out on Saturday. They left everything there except her mom's dresser and their clothes.

Paisley had already been burglarized at the house she was living in, in three separate occasions, and she was convinced her ex-husband was the culprit. She just had no proof.

They moved into a town house, and they were so happy. They literally had nothing in the house, but it was filled with peace, and that was all they wanted and needed. No more fussing, cussing, and fighting. No more abuse. Just their little family to love one another every single day!

By the grace of God, she had her soon-to-be ex sign all the divorce papers by deceiving him a little. She asked God for forgiveness later! Stop judging (wink). Otherwise, he could have made her pay him spousal support and gotten half of her 401(k), and trust me, he would have done just that! He already had her house and vehicle.

What on earth! I didn't know men did that to women. Paisley was literally in shock after talking with her lawyer. She told her lawyer that she would get the papers back to her within a day. The lawyer laughed and said good luck. Paisley looked back and said, "I don't need luck. I have God on my side. See ya soon!" They both laughed for two different reasons, I'm sure!

She called her soon-to-be ex over and asked him if he wanted to save their marriage. He said that he did. She proceeded to ask him to sign all the places highlighted in yellow so that they could get counseling. She still laughs inside because he signed every last place on about twenty pages of documents! It was hilarious!

She knew it was wrong to deceive him, but it was also wrong for him to throw out his own children and try to get her to pay him spousal support after she left him an SUV and the house.

The judge gave him one year to have the house transferred into his name. Do you think that happened? Nope, it went into foreclosure. Her dad saw it in the newspaper! The house payment was only $583.56. She was paying almost double that for the town house! Through all that, she still had peace and joy.

CHAPTER 16

Being A Single Mom Trying To Date

Bam was so happy to be out of that marriage. She wasn't even thinking about dating—ever! Initially, her ex would pick up the children every other weekend. He only lived seven miles away.

Her beautician was so excited for her. You know beauticians are the closest things to counselors that most women have. She was like, "I'm going to hook you up with my fine cousin from Dallas!"

Bam was like, "No, that's okay. Really, I'm super happy being single." She was telling the truth.

Of course, the beautician gave her cousin Bam's phone number. We had cell phones by then, and so he called her. The kids went to bed at 9:00 PM until their senior year of high school, which was changed to 10:00 PM.

It was after their bedtime, so she figured there was no harm in having a conversation. They talked for hours! He was a breath of fresh air. Bam had no idea what he looked like, and she honestly didn't care. She just enjoyed their nightly conversations about his day, her day, their children, life, and just whatever. There was never a dull moment on the phone.

She started feeling like it was high school all over again. She was like, "You hang up!" And he was like, "No, you hang up!" Then they'd agree to hang up at the same time and be like, "Why didn't you hang up!" It was the happiest she had been in years.

Mind you, she hadn't had time to heal from all the brokenness from childhood, which led her to get married at nineteen in the first place, so here she was, more broken and falling for a man whom she had never met! (Red flags everywhere!)

That's what happens when you don't know your worth and how much you mean to God! She didn't realize it at the time, but she, like most of us, was still looking for love and validation from a man that could only come from God.

It truly amazes me how we can be so oblivious to our brokenness and bruises stemming from childhood, even though we had such close relationships with Christ. But that's how the enemy operates. This is why the Lord tells us to renew our minds daily with his Word and meditate upon his promises. I've learned to pray for his promises, not my problems, for real results.

Again, had I not gone through all that mess, I wouldn't have a book to write. Prayerfully, this will help a lot of young ladies and women.

God said it would if I was totally transparent, and he had a lady, an earth angel, come up to me and say, "You really need to write that book God told you to write. A lot of girls will be helped." He would do the rest! I believed him!

That was in 2018, so here I am, writing a tell-all book about our pitfalls and being blinded by the lies of love through the deceit of Satan and brokenness from childhood that was never healed.

Bam talked on the phone for months before they decided to meet. They lived several hours apart. So on one of the weekends that the children were with their dad, they decided to meet each other halfway.

They met early on a Saturday so that they would have time to talk and see if there was any connection. He was six feet four, built like a brick house, and she was completely intimidated. He couldn't tell, but she was so nervous that she was literally having anxiety. She hadn't been on a date ever!

Their date was going well, but she was just so nervous she made up a story to go home. He accused her of making that story up, and since

Bam didn't want him to think she was a liar, she kept lying, saying she wasn't lying! Really!

So she lied and continued to lie to prove that she wasn't a liar. Let us bow our heads and pray for my dear friend. As a matter of fact, pray for all broken and bruised women who don't know their worth or purpose. Amen!

Looking back, he was really a great guy. He just lived too far away and had so many women coming at him. I mean, he was handsome and owned his own barbershop and salon. Who wouldn't want him?

Well, of course, Bam wanted him to be the one. She recalled one time he asked her if she had gained a few pounds. That kicked her in the gut all the way back to childhood again.

She literally lost about twenty pounds in two weeks! She exercised constantly and barely ate anything. He complimented her on how beautiful she looked when she saw him again two weeks later. He definitely liked the new thinner version of her, but we told her that she looked like a crackhead! Honesty is the best policy when you see your friend headed down a path of emotional and mental abuse.

That's another thing: when you don't know who you are or whose you are, you will literally morph into whatever the object of your affection wants. At least, I did. Hopefully, most of you are smarter than I was.

Bam met his family and he met hers. Everything was going great until New Year's Day 2009. She was at church all day, praising God for everything and asking him to reveal anyone in her life who shouldn't be there. She wasn't talking about the object of her affection. She was talking about women who tried to befriend her or anyone except him, because he was obviously the one.

She couldn't wait to call him after church. He sounded elated to hear from her, as he always did, and she felt the same. Then he asked her to hold on for a second because his brother was calling. Of course, she agreed! It was quiet for about two minutes, and then suddenly, she could hear their conversation!

She didn't know if he meant to or not, so she just sat there and waited. Then his brother started talking about some other girl he was messing with who had a husband! Apparently, the husband was harassing him, and he had to go to the police department to file a restraining order. Bam just hung up and fell to the ground and cried.

Apparently, the ground is where we all felt best during our breakdowns, which we seemed to have so often. If you don't repair and get whole, you will continuously make the same mistakes. You'll date the same guy, except he will have a different name, but the same outcome is inevitable.

Bam cried for hours. She cut her phone off. She was finally able to tell us what happened. She could not believe he could lie to her like that. He promised that he'd never lie to or cheat on her, and she believed him.

Why would she not? She was faithful. It wasn't even hard. She couldn't understand what was wrong with her. She was convinced there was something wrong with her and no one would ever be true to her or love her because she was unlovable (the lie Satan has been whispering in all our ears since we lost our innocence as children).

CHAPTER 17

Sasha's Heartbreak

When you're not whole and confident in who you are in Christ, you will find yourself jumping from one relationship to another, trying to get love and validation. The only thing you end up with is a broken heart without the Lord. Only God can fill that void, that deep yearning we have for unconditional love. No man or woman can take on that task. It's too much and will literally drive them away. Don't be desperate when you're a queen. Know your worth, and never sell yourself short for fake love. Having relationship after relationship with hardly any time between them is a sure sign that you're insecure, desperate for love and validation, and feeling worthless if you're not in a relationship—even if it's a toxic, unhealthy one.

Yeah, you need Jesus, not another relationship that is certain to fail. Sasha met a guy literally four months and eight days after her breakup with the last "one." She was seriously not trying to date at all, for real (she said).

One of her coworkers was getting married, and she decided to go to the wedding, but she most certainly was not going after the bouquet. She didn't even try to get cute or anything. She really didn't want to attend, but she didn't want people to think badly of her for not going.

Remember, it's another curse when you don't know whose you are or who you are; you certainly don't love yourself, and you try really hard to please everyone—yeah, that's called being a people pleaser. Never ever do that! Don't swim an ocean for people who wouldn't jump over a puddle for you.

With that being said, Sasha got up and literally picked up some pants off the floor in her closet and put on a shirt with a green blazer. It was nothing glamorous at all.

Remember, the enemy is always looking for a way to get into your life and wreak havoc so that you don't get close to God. That means you might actually figure out how much God loves you and realize that you don't need anyone but God. We should not chase guys. It clearly says in the Bible: "When a man finds a wife, he finds a good thing." There is nowhere in the Bible that says a woman should go out and find a husband. He might be someone's husband, but not hers. Definitely don't do that, because it will always come back to haunt you. Everything done in the dark will always come to light. You're worth more. Never settle for second place. You're a queen!

Sasha arrived to the wedding and mingled with other coworkers while they waited for the wedding to begin. After the wedding, everyone moved over to the reception.

The bride made her way over to Sasha to introduce her to her brother. Sasha was not at all in the mind-set or heart-ready to meet anyone, and she knew that in her head.

That was when it happened! Her life would be forever changed at that very moment. Once the bride's brother turned around to meet her, she literally saw stars floating around his face. Of course, that was before her medication, so we determined it was her crazy alert, which we had all learned to ignore. Never ignore your intuition about a person.

She sat there and talked to him until the reception room was empty and people were cleaning up. It was as if no one was in the room but them.

There was something different about him than the others she had always been attracted to. He wasn't even her type. She was always into tall athletic guys, basically muscular jocks. (That explains how foolish she was. Never judge anyone based on their looks; you could miss your blessing. Plus, if a man spends all that time in the gym, trust me, it's not just for you.)

In other words, they played either football or basketball their entire lives, and you could tell it. Mostly because they could pick her up, it made her feel skinny! So in Sasha's mind, it was a win-win.

He was not buff at all! But he had kind eyes. He seemed like the most trustworthy guy in the world. Surely this guy wasn't a womanizer or a cheater like all her prior loves.

His family was awesome, and she had always yearned to be a part of a healthy and happy family. She was getting everything in one package—the perfect guy with the perfect family! That was it. She was in love, and this one was the one for real!

By the time Sasha met him, she had no games to play. She told him that her boobies weren't really that big; she was wearing a push-up bra. She told him about her past broken relationships. She also told him that she didn't want to have children. She saw no reason in wasting either of their time.

She was sure she'd run him off by being so blunt, but he stayed. He said he didn't want children, and of course, she believed him. (I mean, it was not like she had been lied to by every guy she had ever met and learned nothing, apparently. Remember, you attract who you are, not who you pretend to be.)

They started dating immediately. (No surprise there; her nickname within our group was Needy Nancy.) She said that she wasn't into games, right? Unfortunately, she still had the mask on and was simply unaware. She had worn it since she was a child. She displayed the same traits that she always did. You know, the "I'll be whoever you want me to be because I don't know who I am" trait. (And she had a relationship with Christ! She could help everyone except herself.)

He actually wanted to read the Bible with her and pray with her. He initiated it. Now that was different! He had to be the one, right? But like I said earlier, the Holy Spirit will always give you a warning! We can either be obedient and save ourselves from a lot of hurt and pain or ignore his voice and sign up for a journey of pure hell on earth.

One day, they were sitting there watching a movie, and she just burst into tears! He was like, "Sasha, what's wrong, sweetheart?" And she said, "You're going to break my heart." He was her knight in shining armor for about six months before she saw the "clown with a crown" side. The clown with a crown was who he really was.

She thought the one she met was who he really was, so she decided to wait it out. Surely the one would come back eventually, right? Wrong!

She was already baited and ready to be fried. She literally jumped through hoops trying to please that man. We could all see that he obviously wasn't for her. But you know how petty we can be as women. She accused us of being jealous of what she had. I was like, "The only things that you have that I don't are stress headaches, wet pillows every night, and a purse full of medicine for depression and anxiety."

Honestly, God told her to leave him alone or he would kill her about a year into their situation-ship. She already felt worthless, so she didn't worry about dying. She'd already tried to take herself out, and that didn't work. Now this is the super stupid part! I know, this sounds completely insane even as I type. I'm so glad God is so awesome and merciful. He definitely takes extra care of babies and fools!

She loved his family so much. She felt like they were her family. They dated several years! Yeah, desperate chicks really know how to hang on to someone they know they aren't supposed to be with. She even told him.

That was the other thing; they were more like best friends. People used to think they were siblings the way they carried on. Honestly, that was the part she enjoyed the most. He was an amazing friend. Mental note: If we're not grounded in Christ wholly, not knowing how to love ourselves, we will go out of our way to try and make a temporary relationship a permanent one.

We had never witnessed Sasha try so hard to please someone. I think that was why it lasted so long. She was determined to make him happy. He was a challenge. She had never had that before. Being raised by a man left a few traits in her because guys are the ones who usually love a challenge, I thought.

CHAPTER 18

Sasha's Inevitable Mental Breakdown

During one of their many breakups, I literally witnessed Sasha lose her mind. No, like she was out of her mind for real. I told the girls, and we just didn't know what to do! She practically had no family, and she was not listening to us "haters."

She met some guy on a professional networking site, and after meeting him once, they were in a relationship on social media! That was the dumbest thing ever! Don't worry; it gets so much worse as the story goes on.

The saddest part for me is, no one in her family tried to help her! Not even her dad! She'd tell us that she was driving to an unfamiliar city to meet a guy we've never met, and her dad was like, "Be careful."

Seriously, she was not herself at all. It was very noticeable. I would think her church family or someone other than us "haters" would try and talk some sense into her. She was dating some guy whom no one had ever seen and getting hundreds of congratulations on social media! She said that it was all a blur.

The Lord brought it back to my memory just so I could share with you! Everything happens for a reason, so please know it could happen to anyone.

Now, it's about to get really crazy (do not judge her; she was mentally ill for real). Bless her crazy little desperate heart. I can say that because I've had my share of crazy moments—but let's not get into that.

So what had happened was, she thought this guy was perfect for her. I mean, (he said) he loved the Lord, mentored boys, played basketball—everything her ex did. I think somehow, in her mind, she thought he was her ex!

This is hard to talk about because this really happened, and she could have been killed or something, and no one would have known where she was. That just proved that she didn't matter to anyone and was unlovable once she came to her senses.

Maybe it was the third week of their no-one-knows-what-to-call-it-ship, and he proposed to her! Of course she said yes! This proved that someone did love her, and she was determined to marry him.

After she had the ring and everything, she headed somewhere but didn't know where! She suddenly had no idea where she was or where she was going. She just knew she was on a highway! She started freaking out, so she called me. She said, "I'm literally on the highway, and I have no idea where I am or where I'm heading!"

I calmly replied, "You said you were going to meet that guy you're dating. It's Sunday, so you're probably headed home. Are you being serious right now?"

That was all she could recall from our conversation; however, it did jar her memory. She had flashes on what was happening in her life. She realized that she was engaged to a complete stranger, so of course, she had to break it off because they were strangers. She felt terrible. When she arrived home, she called him and told him that she would mail the ring back to him if he provided his address. That's right; she had no memory of his address! She mailed the ring back, we hope. She blocked him from everything after that because she felt like a mental patient!

Of course, she deactivated her social media account. I'm pretty sure they were still getting congratulations on either their relationship or engagement. I'm really not sure. All I knew was those people weren't her real friends.

Sasha decided that it was time for her to see a new doctor. Her primary care physician, whom she loved dearly, referred her to a psychiatrist, whom she also knew and loved dearly.

My understanding is, you basically try different medicines until they find the one that works for you. That's pretty scary to me, but she obviously needed something.

The first medicine she tried took away her bubbly personality. She was literally walking around in a daze. Obviously, that wasn't the one for her. I can't remember the names, but she went through all of them. Thankfully, the last one worked.

I have to tell you about the one before it. My point is that these medications are serious, and if you're on the wrong medicine, it could cause serious side effects, like death, hallucinations, and the ability to not know what's right from wrong! Basically, the commercials are true.

There is nothing wrong with medication. I also have a therapist, whom I love.

Sasha recalls driving home from work, and there were kids playing in the street. They made no attempt to move. So then she had a conversation with herself over whether or not she should run them over! Thank God for the Holy Spirit. She made a phone call to me, of course, and asked me if she should run over the kids. I can't tell you what I said because it was rated R!

The good news is, she didn't hit the children! When she arrived home, she poured every pill down the toilet! She was crazier than she had been before. Well, it might be a tie. I mean, she did get engaged to a stranger and had no recollection of her life for three weeks.

That's neither here nor there. The point is, you have to be extremely careful if you do decide to take medicine. Some of us need it, obviously, and I'm not ashamed. The messed-up part is when her ex called her, laughing about the engagement. He literally said, "I knew you were going to lose your mind!" Who does that? A clown with a crown!

After all the hell she had gone through since childhood, it was a wonder she didn't lose her mind way before that. Actually, I can say the same for all of us! Life is hard when you are not whole and you are bruised, with no self-love or worth. You can't truly love anyone if you don't first love yourself. So all those relationships that we were in were really nothing but placeholders for Christ. His love is the real deal; agape love is unconditional.

CHAPTER 19

The Move In With Annie's Ex

Annie's first love came back into her life again in 2015. In 2016, he talked about loving her and wanting to marry her. He even said it in front of his family, so of course, she believed him. Why wouldn't she? He proposed with a five-karat ring. It was real. We checked. That's how real friends roll. He had her hooked on the line that would eventually sink her.

After going back to him again after almost fifteen years and after moving into a luxury apartment that was almost double Annie's house payment, they called it quits! The things we do for love when we don't love ourselves or know even half of our worth to God!

So they became roommates, but it was horrible. He would play with her feelings. Some days he would act as if he was totally into her. Then suddenly, he would be gone until late. This went on for months. Annie knew he was seeing someone else. I told you, intuition is never wrong. He lied and said he wasn't, but Annie knew better. Being in a toxic relationship will literally give you bad health. She ended up being diagnosed with vaginal cancer in 2016.

She was distraught and went home and told him. His response was, "Are you sure it's not an STD?" What on earth! He was the one cheating, not her. He was the best at deflecting and a true narcissist.

She removed him from the lease. That's right; she ended up paying this huge payment by herself that was in the middle of nowhere, but only one mile from his job. He had picked that home.

By the way, due to her disobedience to God, everything that she had in storage was stolen! Her things were literally there for three weeks. They had her card on file and autopay. We figured it out. The owner of the storage facility was into heels, just like Annie, and she wanted them. Annie recalls the owner asking her what size she wore, and it was the same as hers! Well, knock me down and call me stupid! How about take the heels but leave the things that she could never replace, you demon. They took her baby pictures with her mom, pictures of her mom, her mom's class ring, and her mom's dresser, which she had carried around all her life. It was horrible. But Annie had no business moving in with him, and she knew it.

The worst part is, nothing was done about her stolen property! She had insurance on her things, but when she called to make a claim, they literally said that she could not do so because her things were "taken, not stolen." That's one of the most ridiculous things I've heard to this day.

Guess what? The insurance company was run by the storage facility responsible for "taking," not "stealing," her life's properties, which can never be replaced. She lost over five hundred pairs of heels! The police told her to get a good lawyer. Someone should have gone to jail. They even told the police that they took her things! Annie retained a lawyer, and two years later, she hasn't heard from anyone. God said vengeance is his, so we pray for them if they're still alive. Don't mess with God's children. He loves us so much that he will literally fight our battles!

CHAPTER 20

Toxic To The Max

I'm not sure if you've noticed or not, but none of us were ever single very long. That's a huge cry for "Help, I'm broken and bruised!" Mind you, we hear Satan whispering to us all day and night that we're worthless, fat, and ugly, and no one will ever really love us! Yeah, we all still believed the enemy's lies. He'd been convincing all of us of the lies through things that were said or done to us as small children. No child should endure such torture.

One night, Flores goes to a class reunion. As she's sitting there, in walks a guy she hadn't seen in years! He looked exactly the same, and apparently, she did too because they called each other's names!

They're sitting there, overdrinking and just catching up. He tells her about his ex, and it was worse than what had happened to her, except it had just happened that day!

Remember, you attract who you are, not who you pretend to be. On the outside, they both looked confident and happy. So guess what? When two needy people come together, it's like fireworks! You'd think she would have learned something from Sasha's social media disaster. But pooh, no. Two weeks later, they're in a relationship! Yeah, another huge mistake!

They pretty much broke the internet because how likely is it that two people who grew up together would reunite at a class reunion and end up falling in love? Blah blah blah. It was a farce. He was an awesome guy, but she knew they were too much alike! She tried to help build him up by telling him how awesome and handsome he was and how he really didn't need anyone but Jesus. He didn't want anything to do with church, so you know that was her exit.

I have to give kudos to Flores. Once she sees something going left, she goes right out the door, closes it, and destroys it. Once she's done, there's no looking back. (Remember, a hungry heart will eat anything. Never go looking for love; you will find everything but that. I know!)

CHAPTER 21

It's A Hard-Knock Life For Some

Obviously, we have learned our lessons the hard way. I'm writing this book about our jacked-up life choices because my Savior told me to, and I'm obedient! My prayer is that someone learns from our mistakes and avoids forty years in the wilderness, like Moses and the Israelites!

Transparency is healing. Everyone thought I was the happiest chick around. I played the part well. Most of the time, I didn't realize I was doing it because it was my default personality. That's gone now. I could not be fake!

I tried it once, and it was so obvious. Whomever I was talking to was like, "You're lying!" and I was like, "You're right! I feel like cutting myself!" And we would laugh! It felt so freeing!

I hate that some of the relationships ended on a bad note. I pray for all of them and their families to this day. I have no ill will in my heart toward anyone. I am filled with God's love, and I can truly say I have never been happier or had more peace than I do now.

CHAPTER 22

Facing Death

So it's time for me to go get my yearly exam, and I'm told that I have a lump in my breast. My primary care physician had a very concerned look on her face, and now I'm freaking out. She can't play anything off, part of the reason why I love her.

She sends me to a specialist the same day while she sends my Pap smear off to the lab. The specialist is concerned too, and I basically take all kinds of tests. Now they're checking to see if it's malignant (cancer) or benign.

While I'm waiting on that, my PCP's office calls and asks me to come in. Are you kidding me? I had lost a ton of weight without trying. I was just unhappy, broken, not mended, and not sure if I had cancer! I hate cancer. People suffer so much, and it breaks my heart.

I get to my PCP's office, and they tell me that they've found cancerous cells and need to do more testing! At this point, I've lost it. I'm convinced that cancer is eating me up. (Remember, watch what you think about because you can bring it about! The Bible says, "There is the power of life and death in the tongue.")

So I tell my young men that I have cancer, expecting them to break down, but they didn't! They were in total denial. They were both like, "No, you don't, so stop saying that. You sound crazy!" I told them to look at me because I was half the size that I was six months ago without trying!

I cried my eyes out all the way back home. I went upstairs into my office, and I lay on my face. I gave up!

I was tired of wanting love and never having it and feeling as if no one really cared about or even loved me (another lie from the pits of hell).

CHAPTER 23

The Awakening

For the first time in my life, there was nothing I could do to fix this. There was no lie. There was no man who could help. And I was ready to die. I cried over everything I had held in over the years! I wish I had cried more growing up. Crying is your body's way of letting out the pain. All the pain, insecurity, self-hate, not feeling good enough, losing my mom, thinking of all the horrible things that was said and done to me by many people for years and years who were supposed to love and protect me, and last but not least, accepting my grandmother's death. With a sincere heart, I cried out loud to God and said, "God, I'm so tired of hurting all my life! I know I have a purpose. Please show me how you see me through your eyes!"

At that moment, I can't explain to you what I felt in human words, but it was as if God gave me a hug! I felt more love than I can describe, starting from the top of my head all the way down to my toes! It was a truly amazing experience! That's why I call it the awakening, because it was like my spirit was asleep before or as if I had blinders on my entire life and Christ removed them in an instant! For the first time ever, I looked in the mirror and didn't see a disgusting girl! I know people always gave me compliments, but I really thought they were only trying to be nice. I'm not vain or anything, but I looked in the mirror and was like, "Girl, you are cute!" I didn't know at the time that God healed me physically, mentally, emotionally, and spiritually!

CHAPTER 24

The Real

Those lies that Satan had been whispering to me all those years fell on deaf ears! I knew who I was in Christ, and nothing could change that, especially not that evil devil who perplexed me since I was a small child.

For the first time, I had real confidence. I felt great! I didn't need validation from anyone. I knew how much God loved me, and that was all that mattered. That was enough to make me feel like I was finally enough and unashamed.

There were side effects to the new me though. I could no longer be fake! I was no longer the entertainer. This is who I had been my entire life. What would people think? It didn't matter. I knew who I was and whose I was, and I started preparing for the divine destiny that God placed in my heart in 1999.

Yes, it still seems impossible, but we know that all things are possible through Christ who strengthens us. Things were looking great. I was studying the Word every day, praying every day, and being obedient to the Lord's will.

Sometimes I would post personal things on Facebook that I didn't want to share (kind of like this book), but if the Lord told me to do it, I did. I have never regretted anything that I've posted. At least one person has always let me know that they were blessed or encouraged by my transparency about my own hardships and flaws.

I call it being flawesome. It means you have accepted your flaws but still know you're awesome. I was never going to go down that road of lies again. No one is perfect, but God. That's why he had to come to this earth, borne by a virgin, planted by God into her womb, to be the sacrifice for us. Otherwise, all of us would be hellbound. Now that's agape love! He loved us while we were still sinners! That gives me the chills. That's the love I was looking for all my life, and he was right in my face the entire time.

CHAPTER 25

Satan's Wrath

Now I'm living my best life with no worries. No desire for any relationship other than Christ. I am simply happy with me for the first time in my life. Actually, I had to make sure I got out of the house to go to church, mentor, and the gym; otherwise, I could easily turn into a hermit! I would have never believed that. I was so needy before. When I think back now, it's hard to believe I was ever that way. That's how much God changed me in an instant.

Don't think the enemy is just going to leave you alone because you've had an awakening and are confident and not on the prowl for a relationship. He will send someone who seems harmless and has a true heart for God. (That's why I pray for supernatural discernment daily.)

Satan has been doing his job well for thousands of years, so without God, we will lose. I hate to admit it, but I had become prideful. It was as if no one could tear me away from my walk with God because I was so strong. Wrong!

I ended up engaged to a guy after about three weeks. I knew the man God had for me would be a preacher or teacher because his purpose would match my own. I also knew the man God had for me would be filled with the Holy Spirit and have a deep and strong relationship with Christ. The more this guy talked, the more I was beginning to think he might be the one. I mean, I am so close to God, and no one could fool me because I have had an awakening, and that was all to it.

I found myself spending more time talking with him than talking to God.

That's how it happens. Slowly, over time, you become lackadaisical, and boom, you're back in the enemy's clutches!

So I began to pray. I didn't know what it was, but something wasn't right inside my spirit. I asked the Lord to have his way. Four days before I was supposed to get married, my jaw locked! I've had TMJ for years but never had a problem getting my jaw shut. The longest it was locked was a couple of hours. I used a surgical mask to lessen my chances of catching the flu or some other disgusting germ (I hate germs of any kind). I went to a chiropractor. That was a horrible mistake! Those manipulations made the pain go from a 5 to an 11! I ended up at the emergency room the same night. They couldn't get my jaw shut. They gave me shots, took all kinds of x-rays, and sent me home with instructions to go see my dentist. Of course, I was going to see my dentist! I would have gone the day it happened, but they were closed.

Now it's three days until the wedding. I asked the Lord to have his way. I should have been more specific about how he should do it. I mean, I didn't think I would end up having surgery the day before the wedding!

After that, I had to have a bilateral arthroplasty. This was a very invasive surgery, and I didn't realize how hard it would be to bounce back. I lost my hearing for a few months. I had two black eyes for weeks. My entire head was the size of a football. They shaved my hair. I think that was the worst part! Excuse me, I need my stylist in here. You can't shave the sides of a chick's hair off without warning! OMG! I still get anxiety when I think about it. I have a short haircut already, but God! Honestly, I can barely see the scars on either side!

During this time, we both came to the realization that we weren't meant to be. There were no hard feelings. Honestly, it was the easiest breakup I've ever had. Maturity and having a relationship with Christ on both sides were definitely blessings.

I love his family, and we're still close. I believe God brings people into our lives for a purpose. Just because it didn't work out between us doesn't mean that his family and I are enemies. That's not displaying the love of God. God is love. We are called to be a light in this dark world, and I don't want to let my Savior down. I am no longer bound by what people think. I only care about what God thinks. As long as I please him, I'm winning!

CHAPTER 26

The New Beginning

After that, I was seriously determined not to date again. Honestly, I could sign up to be a nun today, but I'm not Catholic. Everyone tells me not to say that, but when you've been through toxic relationships from childhood to four decades later, you're literally over it if you have even a little bit of common sense.

I realized that I still had some wounds that needed to be mended because I went from being super humble for the majority of my life to prideful within months!

That's why the Lord tells us to renew our minds daily! The enemy is constantly looking for ways to catch us slipping. I've learned that the closer I walk with Jesus, the more I'm able to see the enemy coming from a mile away.

I have a daily appointment with the Lord now. No matter what, I spend time reading his Word, meditating on it, encouraging others when I can, and praying for this world and all believers to be the salt of the earth, as God called us to be.

God uses others to bless us. That's why I try to do things to help people instead of saying, "I'll pray for you."

A guy who is a mentor to my sons, and actually grew up in the same small town as I did, ended up coming by and brought flowers. I thought that was kind. He then advised that he would cut my grass (it obviously looked horrible). I offered to pay him, but he wouldn't hear of it. So there are still some good people in this world.

I was off work for two months. During that time, I noticed the water wasn't as hot as it should be, so I called the gas company. I thank God that I did because they found a leak, and carbon monoxide was actually coming into the house! There is no telling how long I was being poisoned, but God kept me! I'm telling you, God is faithful, and when he starts a good thing or gives you a vision, he will ensure that he sees it come to fruition as long as we do our part. Meaning, we need to study his Word daily, die to our own selfish needs and wants daily, and pray for his will, not our own. I have learned to walk by faith and not by sight.

CHAPTER 27

The Move

The house was simply unsafe and began to literally fall apart. I prayed, and the Lord told me to move to Atlanta! I always said that I would never live in Atlanta, and all I could do was laugh and say, "Okay, Lord. If you open the door, I'll walk through it."

I tried finding houses in all the beautiful places I knew of but couldn't find anything! Everything I found was literally gone within twenty-four to forty-eight hours. I had no idea Atlanta has been, and still is, growing by leaps and bounds.

God is so awesome. He connected me to a wonderful realtor, who seemed to be more like the sister I never had but always wanted, over the phone! She found a condo for me in an area that I had never heard of, but the Lord told me this was the place. Without even seeing it in person, I told her that I would take it! I went to see it in person a couple of days later, and I loved it! I wasn't crazy about the neighborhood, but I loved the condo.

The realtor and I are sisters now, and I am very close to a church that I've always wanted to attend but was always too far away before. Now it's only thirty minutes away! When God moves you, you'll know because everything will seamlessly flow. I have peace now, and I'm fulfilling my divine destiny.

The Lord told me it was time to get serious about the book. I knew he meant business when a publisher called me out of the blue one day! I was like, "Okay, Lord, I'm not delaying any longer." This book was written in a few months due to some editing issues on my part!

That's another way I know it's God. I have written about so many things that I literally had forgotten about. Every day, before I begin to write, after a full day at work, I would spend time in the Word of God and ask him to give me revelation and recollection of everything he wanted me to share to help other girls and women.

The moral of my story is, simply, God loves you. Say aloud, "God loves [insert your name here] with all his heart and thinks about me constantly!" This is a fact. If you read the Bible, which I call God's love notes to us, you'll see how much he loves you specifically. Once you know that, you'll no longer stay in abusive relationships, you'll no longer need constant validation, you'll be confident in who God created you to be, and he will reveal your purpose to you.

Every believer has a purpose. As soon as we accept Christ into our lives, we are blessed with at least one spiritual gift. Some get several; however, we're all a part of the same body of Christ. Everything truly works out for our good. Had the bad things not happened, I wouldn't be able to warn you about the pitfalls that Satan has in store for you, and I certainly wouldn't be the confident woman of God that I am now. The destiny he has shown me is so big that it scares me, and that's how I know it's going to happen eventually, in his perfect timing! I don't do anything now without God's approval. I don't go anywhere without God's sign-off, and I no longer hang out with just anyone because we have to protect our anointing.

Remember, Satan is constantly looking for a way to take us down or take us out, so don't make it easy for him. As long as you draw near to Christ, he promises to draw near to you and keep you safe! That's a great deal, and one that is definitely worth it. I wouldn't change anything even if I could. Nothing we've been through shall be wasted. My problems aren't for me, and your problems aren't for you. We need to be more transparent with others and help. Don't listen to the lies

Satan tells you. He wants us to keep everything hidden deep inside. That's called bondage, and I've been there for four decades.

Bondage is an emotional, mental, and spiritual prison that keeps your mind unsettled all the time. I finally understand what it means to have peace that surpasses all understanding. Yeah, I'm a slow learner, but once I've got it, I've got it, and I'm going to share it!

Ladies, let's support one another and love one another. We're all either coming out of something, just getting out of something, or heading into something. Let's decide to build one another up rather than tear each down. That is my promise. I am a builder and an atmosphere changer. Join the armed forces for God. When you follow him, you can reap the benefits of living your best life! It's time to thrive, not just survive. Let's do this! Remember, we can do all things through Christ who gives us strength, even write a tell-all book about all your shortcomings, because I promised God that he will get the glory for my story.

Hugs-n-Hersheys!

About the Author

Loco Fab is an anointed daughter of God who is happy to be his servant. She is a mentor with the TN Achievement Program and serves as a mentor for girls eight to eighteen years of age at a local church in Chattanooga. She also started a women's ministry at a different church in Chattanooga that was open to everyone, not just church folks. She has been a guest speaker for multiple events in Chattanooga, Tennessee, and even served as entertainment for an international women's conference.

She is blessed to be the mother of two sons, Henry and Evan. Thankfully and graciously, God had the final say.

She vowed to be obedient to God's voice going forward as she has dedicated her life to his will and is thrilled to be his servant.

It is very true that everything works for the good of those who love Jesus Christ and are called for his purpose. God has mended Loco Fab in all the places she was broken. He will do the same for you!

CPSIA information can be obtained
at www.ICGtesting.com
Printed in the USA
LVHW091925100619
620759LV00001B/1/P